Danny and The Dream Factory

By Steven von Kohorn
Illustrations by David Griffiths

Danny is a little boy that does not like to go to bed. He thinks bed is no fun at all.

In this adventure, through a very interesting series of events, Danny visits the Dream Factory and learns the wonderful secrets behind all of the dreams that we have made for us every night.

Written by Steven von Kohorn, the author of A Tail for Joey and The Adventures of Charlotte & Sparky, this lovely story teaches children that going to bed can be a great adventure and that dreams are very special gifts made especially for them.

Beautifully illustrated by British Illustrator, David Griffiths, the colourful and detailed pictures make this book a treasure that your children will enjoy for many years to come.

If you love Danny And The Dream Factory, be sure to visit **DannyandtheDreamFactory.com** and join thousands of kids receiving their regular newsletter and adventure updates from Active Day Publishing and we will let you know as soon as the next book is available!

Coming Soon! **Danny Saves The Dream Factory**, an exciting tale where Danny is called back to help Chris, Chip and the Dream-Writers save the Dream Factory from the Nightmare Makers.

Enjoy this book! Danny will be glad to have you join him on this adventure and the next!

"Danny! Danny, where are you?" Danny's mother looked everywhere. She looked in all of Danny's favourite hiding spots. She looked in the hall closet. She looked behind the couch. She looked behind the curtains. She looked under the dining room table and in the bathroom. She looked in Danny's room, but she could not find Danny anywhere.

Every night, when it was time for bed, Danny would find somewhere to hide, and his mother would look everywhere for him. Danny loved the game because it was fun but also because he didn't like to go to bed. Danny didn't think that going to bed was fun.

"There you are!" Danny's mother said as she opened the closet door under the stairs and found Danny hiding inside. "Now it's off to bed with you!"

Danny brushed his teeth and climbed into bed. His mother kissed him good night, tucked him in, and turned off the light.

"Sweet dreams, Danny," she said as she closed the door.

"Good night," said Danny.

Danny waited until he heard his mother go downstairs. When all was quiet, he sat up and turned on his bedroom light. He reached under his bed, pulled out a box of toy soldiers, and began to play with them on his bed covers. He set up a pretend battle with the red soldiers on his right and the blue soldiers on his left. His knee was the top of the hill that the soldiers were trying to capture.

Danny's soldiers fought very bravely to capture the hill top, butthey began to grow very tired after a while. Danny too; so soon, his eyes began to close, and his head was nodding. Danny was dreaming of a great battle where he was the general of a powerful army. He was standing on a tree stump and looking across the faces of his soldiers. They listened to him as he planned the battle.

Danny could see his canons shining in the sunlight and his soldiers' bright uniforms.Colourful flags waved in the wind; horses neighed and whinnied in excitement. Danny's trumpeter raised his trumpet and held it, ready to blow the battle call. Danny raised his sword in the air; his soldiers cheered. General Danny was ready to lead his men to a great victory.

Just as Danny was about to shout "Charge!" he woke up.

Danny looked around the room and at the soldiers on his bed and realised he had been dreaming. He began to put his soldiers back into their box when he heard a tiny little voice.

"Oh, dear me, now I've done it. Now I've really mucked things up. Whatever is to become of me...how will I ever get back?"

Danny looked around to see who was speaking in such a little voice, and there, sitting on his pillow, was a tiny man in a blue suit with a pointed hat no bigger than a thimble. In fact, the little fellow was not much bigger than Danny's hand!

"Are you an Elf?" asked Danny. "Or a Pixie?"

"No, Danny, I'm just a silly little fellow who's in very big trouble. Oh, whatever shall I do. How shall I ever return?" The little man said.

"If you're not an Elf, what are you?" Danny asked. "How do you know my name? How did you get onto my pillow?"

"Oh dear, I am in even bigger trouble!" The little man was searching through his pockets, trying to find something.

"What have you lost?" Danny said.

"My keys. I've lost my key to The Dream Factory! Oh, this is very big trouble indeed! Now I can never get back. Oh, this is terrible, this is dreadful!"

The little man pulled off both his boots and shook them upside down. He took off his hat and shook that too. He turned out all his pockets and then began to search around the pillow.

"What does the key look like?" asked Danny.

It's a golden key, and it's very special. It's the only way into the Dream Factory, and I've lost it. Even if I could get home, I couldn't get in. Oh, dear!"

Danny searched around the pillow and under the blankets, careful not to knock the little man off the bed. Then, he looked over the side of the bed, and there on the floor was a very small golden key. It was so small that Danny could hardly pick it up with his fingers. "I've found the key! I've got it!" cried Danny, and he showed the little man.

"Oh, now I can go home. Thank you, Danny." The little man jumped up and danced around the pillow. "Quickly, Danny, give me the key so that I can go back to the Dream Factory."

"What is the Dream Factory?" Danny was looking at the tiny key in his hand.

"The Dream Factory is where all the dreams are made. It's my home. Please give me the key so I can go home."

"Where is the Dream Factory?" Danny asked. "Is it near here?"

"No, no, it's a long way away from here. Well, it isn't anywhere, exactly...it's everywhere."

"How do you get there?" Danny asked excitedly. "Can I come with you?"

"No, you can't come with me, and stop asking all these silly questions. Just give me my key, and I'll be on my way."

"No!" said Danny. "Unless you promise to show me the Dream factory." Danny held the key tightly in his fingers.

The little man sat down on the pillow and sighed.

"Oh, I am in terrible trouble. First, I fall into the Dream Machine, then I lose my key, and I reveal myself to a stubborn little boy who won't let me go home. The worst thing of all is that it all had to happen on my birthday! Oh, whatever will I do?"

"What's the Dream Machine?" Danny asked.

"You ask far too many questions for a little boy. Well, I suppose it is my fault that all this has happened, and I can't blame you for being curious. Alright, Danny, I will tell you all about the Dream Factory, and I will show you the Dream Machine if you promise to keep it a secret."

"I promise!" said Danny, and he leaned closer to the little man to listen.

"No, no, no. You can't see the Dream Machine like that! You have to first lie down and get comfortable. Snuggle into your pillow and relax your whole body."

Danny did as he was told, and the little fellow began to tell his story.

"Well now, where do I begin? Oh yes! Today is my birthday which is a fabulous day for Dream Writers like me. You see, we only have a birthday once every one hundred years, so I was very excited. I decided to make you an extraordinary dream as a sort of birthday present; I knew that you love soldiers and great battles, so I wrote you a great battle dream. Do you remember the dream you were having tonight before you woke up?"

"Yes," said Danny in a sleepy voice.

"Well, that is the dream I was writing for you. Oh, it was lovely! My best dream yet. All the soldiers, the canons, the horses, and the flags. Just when you were about to yell "charge" and lead your men into battle, I became so excited that I fell into the Dream Machine. Instead of the rest of the dream coming to you, I ended up on your pillow."

"Now, I have to get back to the Dream Factory so that I can finish your dream." The little man watched Danny's eyes slowly closing. Danny was almost asleep when the little man whispered into Danny's ear…

"Dream, Danny. Dream of the Dream Factory. Dreaming of the Dream Factory is the secret to going there. Dream Danny, Dream."

Danny fell into a deep sleep. The little man sat on Danny's pillow and waited. Soon, Danny began to dream of a beautiful castle with flags and turrets that reached the sky. The castle was high on the top of a snow-covered mountain, and the whole world seemed to spread out around it.

Around the castle, gates were snow-covered trees and gardens. The castle was as white as snow and had a huge wooden door. There was laughter coming from behind that huge door, and Danny looked up to see other little people in blue suits waving and cheering.

"Oh dear, Oh dear. They are all laughing at me. I do feel like a fool!"

Danny looked around, and there, next to him, was the tiny fellow in the blue suit... only, he wasn't tiny anymore. He was much bigger now. Or was it Danny who had become much smaller?

"Oh well, we had better go inside," he said. He turned to Danny and said,

"By the way, my name is Chip. Welcome to Dreamland, Danny. Come on, I'll show you around."

They walked up to the castle door. Chip put his key in the lock and pushed the big door open. Inside, there was a very long corridor with blue and white stripes on the floor and walls. There was a big blue door at the far end, and Chip and Danny walked up to the door. Chip knocked very loudly on the door, and they waited. Nothing happened. Chip knocked again, very loudly. They waited, but nothing happened this time either. Chip was about to pound on the door when Danny heard someone giggling on the other side of the door.

"Who's there?" a voice said.

"It's Chip. Now stop your teasing and let me in. I have a visitor!"

The door swung open, and another little man in a blue suit looked out at Chip.

"Well, well, Chip. Did you have a nice trip?"

Chip blushed as red as a rose and spoke. "This is Danny. I promised Danny I would bring him to the Dream Factory if he helped me return home."

"Hello, Danny. I'm Pip. Well, this is a treat! We haven't had a boy here for, oh, hundreds of years, I presume. This is exciting. I will have to tell everyone."

And Pip was off down the long corridor calling out to his friends to come and see the visitor.

Danny followed Chip through a series of doors, and finally, they stopped at a very large, bright yellow door with a shiny brass handle. Chip took a deep breath, straightened his jacket, and knocked on the door.

"Come in, come in." a voice said. Chip turned the handle and pushed open the large door.

The room was very big with high ceilings, mountains of books, piles of paper, and lots of brightly coloured boxes. In the centre of the room was a desk, and behind the desk, almost hidden by the piles of papers, books, and boxes, was a rather large, plump, smiling face with long white bushy whiskers and thick white eyebrows.

"Well, well, well. Our traveller has returned. Welcome home, Chip. I am sure that you won't make that mistake again."

Chip blushed again and looked down at his feet. "I'm sorry. I became excited and lost my balance.

"Well, at least you're home safely." The old man smiled at Chip and then looked at Danny. Now don't tell me, this is Danny, the little boy you were writing the dream for. It was a splendid dream, I must say. Were you enjoying it, Danny?"

"Yes, Sir," Danny said, feeling very shy and a bit confused.

"Now, where are my manners?" The old man said as he walked around from behind his desk. "My name is Chris. I am known as The Dream Maker.

Danny looked at Chris and thought he looked very much like Santa Clause.

"You are in The Dream Factory. This is where all the wonderful dreams are made by dream writers like Chip here."

Chris smiled again and put his hand on Chip's shoulder.

"Of course, not all of my dream writers are as talented as Chip, but we are very proud of the dreams we send to people all over the world. Every day and every night, we write and deliver millions of dreams to fill people's sleeping hours."

"How do you make the dreams?" Danny asked.

"Oh, we have a very special machine to do that for us. It's called The Dream Machine. As the dreams are written, they are sent through the dream machine to each person the dream has been written for. Would you like to see the Dream Machine, Danny?"

Danny nodded.

Chris pushed open a huge glass door, and Danny and Chip followed him into a very, very large room. All around this wonderful room were tiers of seats like a sports stadium, and sitting on every seat were Dream-Writers like Chip. They were typing into machines, and beautiful, colourful, exciting, and happy pictures drifted from each machine. There were pictures of unicorns and wizards, great ships and pirates, castles and knights, elephants and clowns, ballerinas and princesses. The pictures glided into the centre of the room, where they flowed down a red and white spiral tunnel.

Everywhere Danny looked, there were more and more Dream-Writers excitedly writing pictures into dreams which drifted into the centre of the room. Every one was different, specially written for a special child, just like Danny.

Chip pointed to an empty seat next to the edge of the spiral tunnel,

"That is my spot, and that is where I fell into the Dream Machine while I was writing your dream."

The images of dreams that poured out of the machine and down the tunnel looked so wonderful and beautiful and happy that Danny wondered where bad dreams came from. He couldn't imagine Chip or Chris writing nightmares or unhappy dreams.

He asked Chris and his face looked sad for a moment before he answered.

"A long, long time ago, some of my Dream-Writers started to write scary and unhappy dreams as pranks. I could not convince them to stop, and one day they just packed up their dream-writing machines and left. Since then, there have been many more unhappy dreams, so I know they have built another Dream Machine and have kept sendingpeople the unpleasant dreams they write.

"One day, Danny, we will find them and stop their bad dreams factory, but for now, we must make as many nice dreams as we can so that there is always plenty of goodness and happiness to share around. We hope that everyone will remember their good dreams and not the bad ones.

"Well, Danny," said Chris. "We better get you home, safe and sound."

"But how will I get home?" Danny Asked.

"You just leave that to Chip. He will write you a wonderful dream that will carry you home and safely into your bed. It has been very nice meeting you, Danny." Said Chris as he turned to walk back to his office.

Danny looked sad for a moment. He really did not want to leave this magical place.

"Come on, Danny," Chip smiled. "I will write you the best dream ever, and I will put all of us in it; the whole Dream Factory so that you will never, ever forget us!"

Danny brightened up at that thought and followed Chip to his Dream Maker desk.

"Just sit there next to me and wait for me to tell you to close your eyes."

Danny sat down and watched Chip rubbing his hands together and then started to type on large magic keys. Pictures of Danny's bedroom started to appear. He was the general of a powerful army in a great battle. He was standing on a tree stump and looking across the faces of his happy soldiers. They listened to him as he planned the battle.

Colourful flags waved in the wind, and horses neighed and whinnied in excitement. Danny's trumpeter raised his trumpet and held it, ready to blow the battle call. Danny raised his sword in the air, and his soldiers cheered. General Danny was ready to lead his men to a great victory.

"Close your eyes now, Danny," Chip whispered.

Danny closed his eyes. He felt his body lift gently from the chair, and he started to drift in the air and move out into the Dream Machine. Then, Danny slowly floated down the red and white spiral funnel. Further and further, he drifted, and he thought he heard a faint voice call out… "Goodbye, Danny. We will always be friends, and I will write very special dreams for you, so be sure to go to bed early."

The voice faded away, and Danny slipped further and further into a peaceful and happy sleep.

The next morning, the sun was shining into Danny's bedroom, and he was still sound asleep when his mother came in.

"Good morning, Danny," she said. "Did you sleep well?"

Danny smiled, sat up and stretched his arms out wide.

"It was the best sleep ever! I think I might go to bed extra early tonight"

If you loved Danny and the Dream Factory, watch out for the next book in this series. Have a look at the other great children's books by this author.

Also, please leave a positive review on the Amazon website so that it is easier for other to find and follow Danny's next adventures.

Your positive review is so important to help books climb the Amazon book index.
Thank you so much for taking the time to leave a review! It leaves the breadcrumbs for others to follow!

If you want to receive an update on the new books in this series, simply visit www.ActiveDay.co.uk and provide your email.
We promise to keep you updated!

Printed in Poland
by Amazon Fulfillment
Poland Sp. z o.o., Wrocław